DUDLEY

AND THE MONSTER

PETER CROSS

Text by

JUDY TAYLOR

G.P. Putnam's Sons
New York

Dudley had slept for a long time. It could have been days, it could have been weeks. Now it was time to see what was happening in Shadyhanger.

Spring had come and
the countryside was
buzzing and busy.

There were squeaks and
snuffles in the bank by the path.

Mrs. Blackbird called a greeting to Dudley as she flew off to find worms for her babies.

Others were on the look-out for food, too.

"I think I'll go and meet those young blackbirds," thought Dudley.

The nest was lined with dry grass and feathers. Dudley slipped in beside the chicks. His eyes began to close...

Dudley woke with a
start as the blackbird babies
flapped and squeaked with
excitement. There, staring at
them, was a monster with
two enormous eyes.

Dudley stood up.
What could be the matter?

Suddenly the monster's nose
began to twitch.

ah...ah...ah...

...tishoOO!

There were feathers
flying everywhere.
The monster shot off
like a dark streak.

When Mrs. Blackbird
came home Dudley and
the babies were playing
"Who can keep a feather
in the air the longest?"

"Goodness. What a busy
morning!" thought Dudley.
"Perhaps I had better go
and have a nap."

"Ah-tishoo!" he sneezed,
and off he set for home
through the falling feathers.